The Night the Barker Burned Down

The Night the Barker Burned Down

The First Book of the Ragamuffin Trilogy

by J.P. Madrox

SENEX
PRESS

Senex Press
Boston, Massachusetts
www.senexpress.org

"We publish the best books."

For Joaquim Maria Nivola

"The fools are not all dead yet!"

*~ Frauds Exposed; or, How the People
are Deceived and Robbed,
and Youth Corrupted*

Contents

Prologue

On the Lord's Day

There are four cornerstones upon which every city is built: the schoolhouse, the courthouse, the marketplace, and the prison. That the graveyard also stands at the foundation of social life is one of those inconvenient truths we conveniently ignore and hope never to have to reckon with. Unfortunately, the forefathers of Boston, in their pious credulity, despoiled those with eyes to see of their willful naiveté by placing the first burial ground so near to the world of commerce that one could not descend upon the city of man without first passing over the dead men's sleepy crest. The hill upon which Isaac Johnson's churchyard sat sloped imperceptibly toward the city center such that the lonely passerby was almost compelled to leave it behind, dragged down by the force of gravity into the mire where all human things meet. This, at least, was what the old, hooded friar thought as he hobbled by its rusted gates and crumbling stone markers, habit dusting the ground in his wake. He paused for a moment in front of the monuments erected nearly three centuries before, stood as if reflecting upon some profound mystery, cleared his throat of its phlegm, and spat. Then he continued on toward Cornhill where the jailhouse slouched in the shade of an old yew and neither rose nor lily dared bloom.

When he reached his destination, the friar removed his sandals and rubbed the dirt from his soft, womanish feet. Standing next to the prison's oaken door, he looked smaller than he was. Not that he was a large man, but the early pilgrims, who understood a thing or two about fear and how it shapes human behavior, had spared no wood when constructing the enclosure and, in the shadow of that daunting edifice, the simple country priest in his simple brown habit seemed all the more minute. He balled his fist against the door with three loud thumps, louder perhaps than would have been expected from so slight and solitary a figure, and the jailer called back from within, "What is it!"

"Open the door," the friar commanded.

"For what?"

"The salvation of souls."

"Ain't got none to be saved in here."

"Well then, for their ruin."

The peekhole on the door slid open and two shifty eyes peered out.

"No papists in here, father," the jailer said and he slid the peekhole shut.

"Now hold just a minute," the friar said. "I was led to believe the keeper of this here inn was a catholic man, albeit not a very strict one."

He pulled two tall bottles from under his cloak and set them on the ground by his feet.

The peekhole slid open again.

"What's this?" the jailer said.

"What's it look like?"

"What's it for?"

"It's for drinking."

"No," said the jailer. "It's for more than that."

"The price of admission, then. I'm told a member of my flock sits rotting behind these rotten walls."

"You here to see the Roman?"

"Who else?"

"Well," said the jailer. "I ain't thirsty enough for that. Ain't fool enough neither."

"Who said anything about a fool?"

"Have to be to let the Roman loose."

"Who said anything about letting him loose?"

"You know what'd happen to me if he got out?"

"I can imagine."

"Well, imagine your way on down the road."

"Now wait a minute," the friar said. "What makes you think I intend to help him escape?"

"Why else would a man in a priest's getup be knockin at my door so early on a Sunday mornin?"

"Come to minister to my sheep."

"Take that hood off and let me look at you."

The friar removed his hood revealing a thick, red mane and shabby red beard, hair masking his face like a veil.

"Where's the man?" the jailer said.

"You're looking at him."

"No. I want to see who's hidin beneath all that fur."

The friar parted his hair in the middle and pulled it back so the jailer could see his eyes.

"What's your name friar?"

"Tuck."

"Friar Tuck?"

"It's what I said."

"What's in those bottles?" the jailer said. "They're sweatin somethin awful out there in that sun."

"These bottles here?" the friar said.

He could see nothing but the jailer's eyes, sallow and bloodcracked from drink.

"These are two bottles of the coldest ale in the city. Just had them filled, right from ole Clem's keg."

The jailer swallowed hard.

"And they're for me?" he said.

"That's why I bought them."

"Go to hell," the jailer said.

"Come now," the friar said.

"You go to hell," the jailer said.

The peekhole slammed shut.

The friar stood in the morning sun. He could hear the chitter of birds in the trees and people coming and going on adjacent streets. There was a horse trotting down the cobblestone in the distance. There were children laughing and somewhere a drunk was singing a jaunty tune.

The bolts on the door unlocked and the door creaked wide on its hinges.

There was the jailer, blinking in the passway.

"They'll hang me," he said, "if he gets loose."

The priest picked up the bottles and walked in.

"Where do you have him holed up?"

Part One

The Night the Barker Burned Down

All he could remember was the sound of the horses screaming. That and the barn engulfed in flames. Hushed voices. Footfalls on dry grass. The red glow of torchlight, flickering, flickering, vanishing in the dark.

"Why are they burning it?" he had asked his mother.

"Because they can."

They abandoned his family's farm that night, grabbed what little they could and made their way through the dark to the road that led to town, embers like so many fireflies dancing in the air behind them. He wanted to stop at the old maple on the edge of the property, the one under which his stepfather was buried. His mother said no.

"We don't have time," she said. "They'll be back."

"Will we be back?"

"No," she said. "Not never."

That was twenty years ago. Twenty years and he had not been home since.

He looked out the window at the blueberry fields as the train rolled past. Half a decade before, the Great Fire of 1903 had devastated the land, clearing out most of the eastern shoreline and leaving miles of charred stumpage around the lake. The blueberries were the first signs of life to spring forth from that destruction and they looked sweet and ripe under the high August sun.

"Next stop, South Rangeley Station," called the conductor. "Then Oquossoc. End of the line."

Morgan stood. He pulled his timepiece from his waistcoat pocket and looked at the time. He read the engraving on the inside cover. *The gods find ways of achieving what we never thought possible.* He closed it and put it back in his pocket, bent down, and pulled a single piece of luggage out from under his seat. A small black box. He held it. Looked it over. Did not open it. Then he put it back under his seat and sat down.

The train pulled to a stop at South Rangeley Station. Morgan watched a fat man and his fat boy exit and walk off toward town, a father and son ready for a week of fishing and bonding by the lake. Another man walked past on his way off the train, a man Morgan had noticed glancing at him on the platform when they were waiting to board. Thick, hairy, donning a bushy black beard and gray bowler cap, the man looked at Morgan through his round rimmed spectacles. Morgan looked back. The man looked away and kept his head down and he did not turn round again. Morgan watched the back of that man's head as he walked off, blending into the crowd and disappearing from sight.

"Yup," Morgan said. "There's Old Scratch himself."

He pulled a pouch of looseleaf tobacco from his breast pocket and packed a thick wad in his cheek. He spat some brown spittle onto the floor of the train and the train started up and rolled out of the station.

"Next stop, Oquossoc," the conductor called. "End of the line."

The Oquossoc Station was the northernmost point on the track. Built at the turn of the century, it was located directly adjacent to an old dirt carry road which serviced the hotels on the eastern shore of Lake Mooselookmeguntic. One of those hotels was the Barker, a secluded resort owned and operated by a Mr. Patton

G.F. Barker, a moneyman who had made his fortune in timber and had spent the better part of the past two decades using his wealth and influence to secure the land needed to extend the railway from Rumford all the way up north to the lake. The Barker was a popular destination for Maine politicians, businessmen, and dignitaries. Countless deals were brokered over cocktails on the beachfront and countless more on hunts in the surrounding wood or while fishing out on the lake. The hotel had a main building with dining, dancing, and some lodging, a casino which opened at noon and remained open until the last of the guests stumbled out early the next morning, and a series of log cabins which could be rented on a weekly basis or for the entire summer and which housed the majority of the patrons. Just behind the camp was Bald Mountain, a spruce-lined hillside where members would hike and picnic. It offered a scenic view of the lake and of the Barker below. The main building, a thirty-five-room mansion, was where Mr. Barker kept his lodgings and it was said that he walked the entire property each morning and every evening with his prized mastiff, a thoroughbred named Marlow.

The train pulled into the station.

Morgan stood and spat.

"Oquossoc. End of the line."

Morgan took his sole piece of luggage out from under his seat, exited the train, and stood on the platform of the station. Next to the station was a water tower and a coal shed and to the left of the tracks was a stockpile of new ties. What those ties were doing there, no one knew; but there were rumors circulating that Mr. Barker was developing more land up by Lake Kennebago and that he wanted to extend the track farther still.

"Need a ride? Or a place to stay?"

A man in a checked cap called to Morgan from the front seat of a livery car.

Morgan sat back on his heels.

"A ride, maybe."

He spat.

"What resort you stayin at?"

"The Barker."

The man gave him a straight look.

"The Barker?" he said. "It's mighty expensive."

"That's what they tell me," Morgan said.

"And," the man said. "Well, sir. It's pretty exclusive."

"So I've heard," Morgan said.

"It's just," the man said. "I'm not sure—" he paused. "It's just—they don't let colored folk in."

"That so?" Morgan said.

The man blushed.

"My daddy, he fought for the union," the man said. "Or at least he would've, if it weren't for his bum knee."

"Right," Morgan said.

"Tell you what, why don't you come back with me?" the man said. "Me and the Mrs., we run a little place not far from here. Mooselookmeguntic House. It's nice enough. Right by the water. We got hot coffee and my wife—she's a real good cook. Fix you up something nice. What'd you say?"

"How much for a ride to the Barker?"

The man looked at him.

"You want to go to the Barker?"

"It's what I said," Morgan said.

"Ok," the man said. "Alright. Well hop in and we'll talk rates on the ride."

Morgan walked over and climbed up into the passenger seat of the livery car and the car started with a kick and set off down the carry road.

"The name's Loamma Lott," the man said. "But everyone calls me Lo."

"Morgan," Morgan said and he spat his brown spittle out the side of the car.

"Morgan," the man said. "Well I'll tell you what, Mr. Morgan, I shuttle a lot a people to that Barker and I shuttle a lot back. And not a one a them looks any better for havin been there. You're supposed to rest when you're on vacation. You're supposed to relax. Though I suppose they ain't the relaxin type. You know what I mean? Guys who work every day a their lives, even when they're not workin. Guys who gotta do somethin to relax—boozin and gamblin and raisin all sorts a hell. Now don't get me wrong, I work just as hard as the next guy. Harder. But Sunday's the lord's day and I'll be goddamned if I don't respect it. I rest on the sabbath because rest is sacred. That's what the good book says. Or at least that's what the Mrs. says and you can't go arguin with her. Try if you like but it won't do you no good. She's thick as molasses. But she can be twice as sweet—when she wants to. Which ain't all that often. Marriage is a foolish thing. Still can't wrap my head around it after all these years. But why am I tellin you? You're married, ain't you Mr. Morgan?"

Morgan spat.

"No? Well, I tip my cap to you. Marriage is a foolish thing. Goddamn stupid is what it is. Course, I'd be lost without the Mrs. I'd be a drunk is what I'd be. You think those hellions up at the Barker raise Cain? They don't know the half of it. When old Lo lets loose, that's a sorry sight. Sorry for everyone else a course. And for me too. Now daddy, he was a drinkin man. And he could fight with the best a them. That's what kept him from seein battle. Supposed to fight under General Howard but instead he got himself into a little tussle and they sent him right back home to Roxbury. Didn't want him anywhere near the battlefield. Which never made much sense to me. You think you'd want the meanest sonsabitches fightin on your side. Though I suppose you best be sure they're on your side. And that's tough to do when they're beatin their fellow companymen half to death. Daddy was never the same. Or at least that's what mama always said. I wouldn't know. I was the youngest of eleven and he was dead before I knew how to shoot."

"That the Barker?" Morgan said as the car rounded a corner and the main building came into view.

"That's it," the man said. "The Barker. Now hold on a minute. I'll drive you right up front."

Morgan took in the property.

It was big, green, smelled of lake water and pine.

"Old Mr. Barker," the man said. "He's got himself a gold mine right here. And he ain't afraid to grease a few palms to keep it that way. I can't tell you how many senators and state reps I drive right through these gates. Not to mention all the lawmen too. Come up from Augusta on holiday and have themselves a time. Run their mouths when they've been drinkin is what they do. Talkin about 'Barker paid so and so to do this' and 'Those folks gotta get out cause Barker wants that.' How you get to be in power when you can't even hold your liquor? That was the best thing daddy ever taught me. How not to talk. How just to listen. And sometimes how to punch. But these big-time boys, they don't know the first thing about it. I may not have their suits or their smarts, I may not've gone to Bowdoin or Bates, and I sure as hell don't have their clean-toothed, hair-combed wives, but I know some things all the same. I know how to shoot and I know how to hunt. I can fix damned near anything and I can make things with my hands. And most of all, I know how to spot a devil. I know his tricks and I know how to run when he calls my name. And I'll tell you one thing more, Mr. Morgan. I know that that Barker is just about the slickest devil ever to set his hoofs in our little town. You have something he wants and he'll take it, just like that. Get mixed up with him—you're goin to get burned. I guarantee it."

The car pulled to the front of the main building and rolled to a stop.

"Well," the man said. "I don't suppose they'll let you stay. But if you want to try, you have at it."

"They'll let me stay," Morgan said.

"How's that?" the man said.

"I'm a guest of Mr. Barker's."

Morgan climbed down out of the car and walked off without paying.

The liveryman watched for a moment and then drove away.

~

As Morgan ascended the front stairs of the main building, he was stopped by a busboy clearing tables on the veranda.

"Can I help you, sir?" the busboy said.

Morgan pulled the brown chaw from the side of his mouth and placed it in the busboy's hand.

"Thank you, kindly," he said.

He tipped his hat and walked in.

Inside, the Barker was buzzing. The dining room was full and there were people laughing and dancing, sipping cocktails and listening to live music. On one side of the room was a long, hand-carved oaken bar and behind it was a mural of a steam engine rattling down the tracks. On the other was a dancefloor where men and their wives or mistresses danced the waltz. At the back of the room, glass windows looked out onto the lake. It was nearly eight at night and the summer sun was setting red over the mountains and the light came in off the lake and lit the room in shades of crimson and gold. A few patrons eyed Morgan as he walked past, but most seemed drunk already, as dead to the world as a few years on they forever would be.

Morgan walked to the bar and sat.

He was there for only a minute when one of the guests approached, a wiry looking man in polished shoes and a neatly tailored suit.

"Hey boy," he said. "What do you think you're doing sitting at that bar?"

Morgan turned.

"Sounds like you answered your own question, friend. I'm sitting at the bar."

"I see that," the man said. "But who told you you could?"

"I didn't ask," Morgan said. "I just sat."

"Get up," the man said.

"That's ok," Morgan said. "I like it fine right here."

"Get up," the man said. "I wasn't asking."

Morgan stood and the man seemed only now to appreciate his size.

Morgan towered over him. His hands looked like they could crush him with a single blow.

"Do you know who I am?" the man said.

"If I did," Morgan said, "I don't suppose it would matter."

The man looked around as if expecting someone to come to his aid.

No one did.

The man lifted his glass to his lips, ice cubes clicking against the rim.

He sipped his drink and peered at Morgan with bloodshot eyes.

"All right," he said. "You enjoy your evening."

"I aim to."

The man walked off and Morgan sat back down.

"You aren't from around here," the bartender said.

"Nope."

"Only two types a people would talk to Eddie Fontane like that. A man with connections and a man with a death wish."

"I don't have no connections," Morgan said.

The bartender laughed.

"We don't usually serve your type, but there's no hard rule. What're you having?"

"I hear old man Barker likes his gimlets."

"You hear right."

"Make one for him and set it right here beside me. I'll take a rye whiskey myself."

"Mr. Barker expecting you?"

"He is."

The bartender gave him a discerning look.

"You're here on business?"

"I am."

Then, in a hushed voice, "Are you the—"

"The Pinkerton man," Morgan said. "Tell him I'm here."

"What name should I give?"

"Agent Morgan," Morgan said. "And tell him I brought what he asked for."

He placed the black box on the bartop and tapped it with his oversized palm.

The bartender nodded and turned to walk away.

"Hey barman," Morgan said.

The bartender turned.

"How about those drinks?"

~

Morgan had finished his whiskey and had started in on Barker's gimlet by the time the bartender returned. No one bothered him as he drank but the woman seated next to Eddie Fontane stole glances at him from across the room. He nodded to her, and she blushed and Morgan said to the bartender, "Some beauty."

"I'd advise against mixing it up with Mr. Fontane, sir," the bartender said. "No amount a beauty is worth that kind a trouble."

Morgan downed the rest of Barker's drink.

"Mr. Barker," the bartender continued, "asked me to convey the following message: We stand at the river's edge."

"Then let the die be cast," Morgan said.

"Very good, sir," the bartender said. "Please come with me."

Morgan rose and followed the bartender back behind the bar to a door that led into the kitchen. There, the waitstaff moved busily to and fro, the cook prepared his area for the next morning's meal, and the busboy from the veranda scrubbed dishes and glared at Morgan with gritted teeth. Morgan tipped his cap to the boy as he walked past and followed the barman out of the kitchen, down a corridor, through a doorway, into a large office with built-in bookcases and a fire crackling in the hearth.

"Mr. Barker," the bartender said. "This is Agent Morgan of the Pinkerton Agency."

Morgan nodded.

Seated on an armchair by the fire was an old man among his books, a solitary figure with a world of learning at his disposal and no one to share it with.

"Agent Morgan," Barker said. "Please sit."

Morgan walked over and sat himself on a chair across from Barker.

Barker's dog sat on the floor beside its master, a mean looking mutt if ever there was one.

It growled at Morgan.

Morgan leaned forward, reached down with his huge hand, and whacked it on the snout.

The dog whimpered.

Barker gave Morgan a startled look.

"I grew up with animals," Morgan said. "Show them kindness and they'll cling to you. Show them power and they'll do what they're told."

Barker smiled.

"Care for a smoke?" he said, and he opened a wood humidor on the table beside him.

"Listen," Morgan said. "I don't have much use for pleasantries. I'm not one of your politician friends. I'm here to do a job. I'm here to do it well. But first I need to know what it is."

Barker nodded. He was a thin man with pale skin and white whiskers sprouting from his jowls. Not at all what you would have expected. He had about him an air of disinterest. He was a man who could buy anything he wanted, but who wanted nothing more than a good night's sleep. Money keeps you awake his eyes seemed to say. And there's no rest until you enter that place where it, like everything else, has lost all value.

"Gabriel," he said to the bartender who was still standing by the door. "Pour Agent Morgan a glass of port and refill mine. Then give us some privacy."

The bartender hurried over to a nearby decanter and did as he was told. Then he made his exit, closing the door behind him.

"Now," Barker said over the rim of his glass. "Let's talk."

"Talk," Morgan said.

"Your agency has run into a bit of trouble of late."

"It has," Morgan said.

"It hurts your credibility. How can people trust the Pinkertons when there are imposters going about pretending to be Pinkerton agents?"

"People are too quick to trust," Morgan said. "They'd do well to be a bit more cautious."

"What you say is true," Barker said. "But I'm not talking about people. I'm talking about me."

"So am I," Morgan said. "Trust me or don't. That's your business."

"My business is your business," Barker said, "when you're in my employment."

Morgan sipped from his glass.

"Is that my package?" Barker said.

Morgan nodded.

"Any inkling what's inside?"

"That doesn't concern me," Morgan said.

"It does indeed," Barker said. "And you'll see why when you open it."

Barker stood and walked over to one of the bookshelves. The wall in front of him was lined with ancient texts, from Homer and the tragedies to Thucydides and Herodotus all the way up through Virgil, Aurelius, Plotinus, and the *Posthomerica*. He took down an old, leather-bound book, returned to his chair, and handed it to Morgan. It was a copy of Plato's *Politeia* in the original Greek.

"What's this?" Morgan said.

"Open it."

Morgan opened the book.

It had been hollowed out and there was a golden key inside.

"Not everything is what it appears to be," Barker said. "Now open the box."

Morgan fitted the key into the lock on the front of the small black box and opened it.

It was empty.

"I don't get it," Morgan said.

"Over the past nine months," Barker said, "nearly a quarter of a million dollars in jewels and paper bonds has been stolen by someone falsifying himself as a Pinkerton agent. Some of that money belonged to my associates. Most of it belonged to me. Yet if you want protection, you won't go with anyone else. Your employer has that kind of reputation and, by and large, deserves it. I've worked with the Pinkertons for many years. I thought I could trust them. But recent events have shaken my confidence and shown me that I need to be more careful."

Morgan grunted.

"The locking mechanism on that box," Barker continued, "has been equipped with a small mechanical device, a device which, should the box be opened by any means save that very key, will release a blue dye, staining both the interior of the box and the hands of the one who's opened it."

"There's no blue dye," Morgan said.

"No," Barker said. "Consider the safe transport of that little box—a box known to be of significance to one of the richest men in New England—a test passed. If you're going to work for me, I need to know I can trust you. And now, Agent Morgan, I feel ready to."

"What do you want me to do?"

"I want you to protect me," Barker said. "I want you to protect this hotel."

"From what?"

"That's what I don't know," Barker said. "That's what you're going to find out. In addition to the recent commandeering of my personal property, I now have reason to believe that my fortune, and maybe even my life, is in danger. Of course, that's how it is for men with power. We're always standing in someone's way. But this time, the threat is more immediate, more concrete."

Barker pulled an envelope from his breast pocket and handed it to Morgan.

"Last week," he said. "I received this. I don't know who sent it."

Morgan opened the envelope.

Inside was a single sheet of yellow paper with the words THE BARKER WILL BURN scratched on it in a barely legible script.

Morgan looked at the old man.

Barker looked back.

Sad eyes, empty and gray.

"There's someone out there who wants to do me harm," he said. "But I can't protect myself if I'm fighting shadows. I need help if I'm going to smoke this devil out. Am I right in thinking that you're the man to help me?"

"That's a nice gun you got mounted on the wall," Morgan said. "Where'd you get it?"

Barker turned and looked at the revolver hanging over the mantelpiece.

"That?" he said. "That's a Colt 1848 percussion revolver. It was originally part of a pair. My father spent some time on the frontier back when it was wild, when its wild men showed you the wilderness of your own heart. It's where my family first tasted fortune. Pa never told me what happened to its twin. Probably didn't know himself. Do you like guns, Agent Morgan?"

"I like what they can do."

Barker smiled.

"You're the man I need," he said. "What do you say? Will you help me?"

"That depends," Morgan said.

"On what?" Barker said.

"In all likelihood, your enemy is here, now, disguised as someone you know, someone you think you can trust. If I'm going to do this and do it right, I need your sanction. I need to know I can do whatever it takes, even if it means offending some of your guests."

"Of course," Barker said. "There are no guests without the Barker."

"Ok," Morgan said. "Then join me at the bar. Show everyone in here that you're not afraid to be seen drinking with a half-indian, half-white, half-colored mixed-up, multiple man. Put your hand on my back. Laugh. Make like we're good friends. Show those rich sonsofbitches that I'm here on your account and that they better not bother if I'm hanging around."

Barker shifted in his chair.

"Well?"

"Of course," Barker said. "Of course, you're right. If that's what it takes."

"Good," Morgan said. "Then I'm your man."

The two shook hands, finished their drinks, and walked back to the bar.

~

"I don't often dine here," Barker said in a hushed voice as he and Morgan seated themselves at a table in the corner of the room. "I only check in from time to time, ask people how they're enjoying their meals, if there's anything we can do to improve their stay. My business is conducted in my own private dining room, and I prefer not to mingle with the guests."

"Even better," Morgan said.

"Port?" Barker said.

"I'm drinking what you're drinking," Morgan said.

Barker called the bartender over and requested two glasses and a bottle of port.

Morgan rose to his feet.

"Excuse me for just one minute," he said.

"Where are you going?" Barker said.

But Morgan was already walking away.

He strolled across the room to the table at which Eddie Fontane sat with his redhaired wife. He patted Fontane on the shoulder, picked up a glass of scotch from the table in front of him, sipped it, and said, "That's nice."

Fontane looked up in disbelief.

Morgan finished the drink, crunched the ice with his teeth, and placed the empty glass back on the table.

"I was thirsty," he said. "I needed that."

Fontane's face turned bright red.

But Morgan wasn't looking at him. His eyes were fixed on Fontane's beautiful, young wife.

"All right," he said. "You two enjoy your evening."

He turned and walked back to Barker's table.

The bartender was standing there pouring him a glass of port.

"Turns out I have connections after all," Morgan said.

"Turns out you do."

~

Barker and Morgan spent the night drinking wine and whiskey, smoking pipe tobacco and discussing the patrons—who they were, where they came from, anything that might help Morgan figure out who was behind the threatening letter. They talked about the employees too, but Barker was skeptical that anyone on his payroll would want to do him harm. He made a point of paying people well, he said, and he never worked them too hard.

"Show your employees that you value what they do, and they'll value doing it. That's always been my motto."

At one point, Morgan excused himself and stumbled drunkenly after the busboy who was exiting out into the night. He caught up with him on the veranda, apologized for their first encounter, asked him a few questions about working for Barker and about the hotel, and handed him a crisp ten-dollar bill. It was more money than the boy would make in a month and Morgan knew what that meant to a poor kid.

"Thank you, mister," the boy said. "I don't know what I did to deserve it."

"Let me tell you," Morgan said.

He whispered something in the boy's ear and returned to the table grinning.

"What was that about?" Barker said.

"I'm a congenial guy," Morgan said. "I like to make friends."

"You're not here to make friends," Barker said. "You're here for my protection."

"There's no better protection a man can have than a good friend."

~

Hours later, when Morgan stood to go relieve himself, it was daybreak. The sun was coming in through the dining room windows and Morgan felt like his legs might give out beneath him.

"How much did we drink?" he said.

"Enough," Barker said.

Morgan stretched his limbs.

"I've had a cabin prepared for you," Barker said. "Number 43. Right next to the casino. Go sleep off the booze and get your head right. I want this matter resolved as quickly as possible."

"How quickly are we talking?" Morgan said.

"I'll pay for however long it takes," Barker said. "But in an ideal world, we'd know who we're dealing with and what he's up to very soon. I've yet to mention this, but I have some important negotiations to work through with one of the patrons and I don't like it when my business gets interrupted."

"Do those negotiations have anything to do with all the land you've been buying up between here and Kennebago?"

Barker gave him a skeptical look.

"You think I'd take a case like this without knowing who I'm working for?" Morgan said. "You think the Pinkertons don't have a file on every moneyman from here to the Rockies? Farther. But all you really need to do is ask down at that train station and people'll tell you: Barker's moving up north."

"People talk all sorts of nonsense," Barker said.

"Maybe," Morgan said. "But sometimes they're right."

"Get some sleep," Barker said. "You've got a job to do."

Morgan nodded and stumbled out.

~

Outside, half of the sky was mauve with the horizon descending into black and the other half was clear and blue, lit up by the first rays of the rising sun. The sun rose steadily over the mountaintops, but the moon was still visible, a great white ball suspended in midair. Morgan walked along the edge of the lake and looked up the beach at the log cabins set back in the green summer grass. Inside were people drunk and sleeping or early-risers readying themselves and their tackle boxes for a day of fishing on the lake. Morgan stopped to watch an old housewife chase the geese off her cabin's lawn. She waved a broom at them and said, "They get their muck all over the yard!" and Morgan nodded and walked on.

As he approached the casino, he heard a commotion coming from out back and made his way up the beach to see what was the matter. There he found two men, Barker employees, holding a third up by the arms. It was the liveryman, Loamma Lott. He was drunk and swaying and he could barely stand.

"You can't keep doing this," one of the employees was saying. "Mr. Barker won't have it."

"He'll have my money!" Lott slurred. "He'll have my land and all my money too, won't he?"

"What's the problem?" Morgan said.

"Who the hell are you?" one of the employees said.

"Morgan," Morgan said. "What's the problem?"

"No problem," the other employee said. "Mr. Lott here was just about to pay his debt and make his way home to his business—while he's still got one."

"Like hell I was!" Lott said and he tried in vain to break free.

"What's he owe?" Morgan said.

"What's it to you?"

"What's he owe?" Morgan said.

"A hundred and seventy-seven dollars as of this morning."

Morgan took a roll of bills from his breast pocket. He counted out two hundred and fifty dollars and threw it on the ground at the employees' feet.

"There," he said. "Now let him go and get back to hustling like Mr. Barker pays you to."

The men glared at him.

"Go on," Morgan said. "Get."

The two men let go of Lott, bent over, begrudgingly collected the bills, and walked back into the casino.

Lott sat down on the grass.

"Thanks for that," he said, and he hiccupped.

"Don't worry about it," Morgan said. "What're you doing up here anyway?"

"What's it look like?" Lott said. "Tryin to take back some a the money that swindler Barker stole from me when he opened this joint."

"You think you're going to get your money back in there?" Morgan said.

Lott spat.

"Tell me," Morgan said. "What do you think of Mr. Patton Barker?"

"I think he's a bloodless leech," Lott said. "I think someone oughtta take him out back and shoot him like a stray dog."

Morgan nodded.

"What do other people think?"

"They think he's the second comin a Christ."

"How do you mean?"

"Look around," Lott said. "He built this whole world. Created it out a nothin. I've been here all my life. You couldn't find a postbox before old man Barker came sniffin round. There's no railway without him. No casino. No hotel. No guests with their fancy clothes and handfuls a spendin cash. No one'd even know this place was here."

"He's been good for business."

"Yeah," Lott said. "His business. He bought up all the land. Tryin to buy up even more. And if you ain't sellin? Too damned bad. Pay you a fair price if you ask him."

"And if I ask you?"

"Listen," Lott said. "I'll tell you somethin, somethin no one will cause no one wants to see. There ain't no creation without destruction. You can't build without tearin somethin down. That's a fact. But people don't like facts. People like ideas. People like feelin good. You know who don't feel too good? Those a us who got crushed. Those a us who got destroyed so someone else could build. Someone like old man Barker, son a Beelzebub himself. We know the facts. We know em cause we live em. And to us, that second comin looks like the will a the world comin to step on our heads."

"Ok," Morgan said. "Let's get you home before your wife starts to worry."

Morgan helped Lott to his feet and the two stumbled their way over to Lott's livery car and Morgan gave him a boost to get in.

Lott tried to pull himself up into the driver's seat but lost his footing and fell right down into a puddle of mud.

"Jesus," he said. "Just my luck. These are my only pants. I split the ass a my best trousers last week."

Morgan started to laugh.

"Now what's so goddamn funny?" Lott said.

But Morgan couldn't stop. He was hysterical.

And, seeing how despondent his situation was, Lott had no choice but to laugh along with him.

"You're a real sonofabitch," he said. "But I'll be god-damned if I don't like you."

"Come on," Morgan said. "Give me the hand crank and I'll drive you home."

"Got anything to drink?" Lott said.

"I might have a touch of whiskey in my flask."

"I'll trade ya," Lott said.

He pointed Morgan to the crank and Morgan handed him the flask and helped him up into the car before walking around front and fitting the crank into the shaft.

"What brings a colored fella like you all the way up here anyway?" Lott said as nestled his face into the windowglass.

Morgan cranked the crank around in a circle and the engine coughed to life.

"Me?" he said. "I'm here on business."

He climbed up into the car.

"And just what kind a business is that?" Lott said.

"The kind that introduces you to cretins like Mr. Barker," Morgan said. "I'm a Pinkerton man."

~

Morgan drove Lott's livery car back to the Mooselookmeguntic House and parked it out front. He left Lott snoring in the passenger seat and went in for a cup of coffee. There, he met Lott's wife, an ugly woman with a good deal of common sense. She made Morgan a plate of runny eggs and buttered toast and said, "My husband's a damned fool."

"He's just a drunk," Morgan said.

"Same difference," she said. "He's been good for nothin his whole life."

"Why'd you marry him?" Morgan said.

"Look around," she said. "Ain't a lot a options way up here."

Morgan nodded.

"Let me ask you," he said. "You think he could ever hurt anyone?"

"Besides himself?" she said. "Nah. He's nothin but a bag a goose scat in a workin man's suit."

"Would he ever threaten to?"

"Lo?" she said. "Sure, he might. He's a talker. Likes to run his mouth. Specially when he thinks he's been wronged—which is damned near all the time."

Morgan sipped his coffee.

"Why'd you ask?" she said.

"Here," Morgan said.

He pulled his money roll from his pocket and counted out five hundred dollars.

"You take this and you drive that dope you call a husband as far from here as you can."

She looked at him.

"We ain't seekin charity, mister."

"It's not charity," Morgan said. "It's protection."

"Protection from what?"

"From a man whose mouth is going to get him and his wife into a world of trouble and he's too goddamned stupid to know it."

She looked at him.

"Where'd a black fella like you get all that money?"

"Thanks for the eggs," he said. "I got to go."

~

Morgan walked back to the Barker on foot. It was a hot August morning and by the time he got there, it was close to midday and he had sweated most of the previous night's liquor out into his socks. He stunk something awful, but the smell didn't bother him. He had a job to do. So he made his way down to the casino, mounted the freshly stained wooden stairs, and, finding the door to the gambling house locked, pounded it with his fist.

"There's no one in there," said the voice of a woman on the porch behind him.

Morgan turned.

"They close at daybreak and the tablemen don't come back to count the money until lunch."

"You know the ins and outs of this place, don't you Mrs. Fontane?"

The lovely redhead smiled.

"I've been vacationing here for years and years," she said.

"You can't be a day over twenty-five," Morgan said.

"Twenty-three this past June," she said. "But I've been coming here since I was still in school. I met Eddie here."

"He hasn't been in school for a long time," Morgan said.

"No," she said. "There's only so much a man like him can learn before he starts teaching people his lessons."

"Is that so?" Morgan said.

"That's so," she said.

"You're pretty," Morgan said. "But you're either too young or too stupid to know what kind of trouble you're going to get in flirting with a man like me."

"That's what you think this is?" she laughed. "Oh darling, you're sweet."

"What then?" Morgan said.

"This is a warning," she said. "I came to tell you before it's too late."

"I'll bite," Morgan said. "Tell me what?"

"Most of the women here," she said, "look at a man like you and see nothing but danger and dark. They see what they want to see. A fiction man. A fantasy man. A man born of their caprice. Anything but their husbands. Anything but those soft, pale gutterfish they sleep next to night after night. You're hard. You're rough. You've got edges. That's what they want to believe. They'd love to have you just one time and then never look at your black ass again."

"What about you?" Morgan said.

"Me?" she said. "I know trouble. I know the kind of trouble that makes men like you flinch. I know the weight of it, how it feels when you're holding it in the palm of your hand."

She pulled a small, black revolver from under her dress and pointed it at Morgan's knee.

"Mr. Morgan," she said. "Patton Barker is not a good man. But he's a rich man. And a useful man. And to some people, even a dangerous man. He and my husband have their arrangements. They aim to tend them.

And anyone who stands in the way of that won't be standing much longer."

There was a rustling in the bushes, but they both ignored it.

"Come now, little girl," Morgan said. "Are you ready to see that promise through?"

"Take this as your warning," Fontane said. "You have my word. One way or another, this mess you're bringing with you ends tonight."

She put the gun back under her dress, turned, and descended the stairs.

"What, no kiss?" Morgan called after her.

But she continued to walk away.

Just then the door to the cabin next to the casino, Cabin 43, creaked open and out crept the busboy, blinking in the daylight. He looked from side to side and, not noticing Morgan on the terrace across the way or the unseen spectator in the bushes, he walked hurriedly up the beachfront toward Bald Mountain.

Morgan observed this without saying a word. Then, once the busboy was out of sight, he descended the stairs and walked over to the cabin that Mr. Barker had had made up for him, pretending not to know he was being watched. He opened the door, stepped in, and closed it behind him. He did not light the lantern hanging on the wall just inside the door. Instead, he stood there in the silence of the room and allowed his eyes to adjust to the dark. When they had, he picked up a piece of stationery lying on the table in front of him. He read it once, folded it, and put it in his pocket. Then he stood there motionless, not thinking, not moving, nothing. How much time passed in that interval is hard to say. But after taking in the room, the stillness of that still, small space, Morgan exited back out into the light and followed the trail along which the busboy had walked. He climbed up the side of the mountain along a windy path, stepping over roots and rocks and moss-grown stumps, and when he reached a small clearing, not at the summit but perhaps halfway up, he noticed broken branches and bent reeds just off the path, and, walking over to take a look, found lying in a little gulch the mangled body of the busboy. He was all crumpled up like a piece of wastepaper might be. Someone had broken his neck.

~

Loamma Lott awoke with a pounding in his head and the taste of cheap cigarette smoke in his throat. It was past midday and the harsh, nasally voice of his wife repeating his full name again and again alerted him to the fact that he had done something regrettable and was about to pay for it.

"What're you yappin about?" he said and immediately wished he hadn't.

What his wife was yapping about was him getting his drunk ass out of the livery car so she could take it over to Rangeley to buy some supplies. And when, without thinking, Lott replied, "Just take the goddamn horse," his wife poured a full bucket of well water on his head and threw the bucket in his lap.

"Jesus, Midge," he said. "Now why'd you go and do a thing like that?"

"You're a good-for-nothing," she said. "And I'm leavin you."

Lott was confused.

He was too hungover, or perhaps still too drunk, to make sense of what his wife was telling him.

"Can't I get a cup a coffee," he said, "and we can sit and talk this over?"

"You're not hearin me, Lo. I'm done. Gone. Now get out a that car."

There were not many things that Loamma Lott was good at, but one of them happened to be refusing to do what his wife said, especially when he was in the wrong.

"I ain't movin," he said. "And just where do you think you're goin anyway?"

"Away from you," she said.

"Away from me," he said. "And with what money? Or do you forget who works around here?"

She laughed a shrill, condescending laugh.

"Don't you worry about my money," she said. "Now get down from that car before I cause a scene."

"Cause a scene?" he shouted. "It's a bit late for that, ain't it?

"That's right everyone," he continued in pantomime, performing for a nonexistent audience. "Take a good look over here. Ole Loamma Lott can't even keep his woman in check, so busted out is he. Now she's goin to leave him to do whatever she damn well pleases with whoever she damn well pleases—with what money? no one damn well knows—and all because he ain't goin to move his sorry ass off a this goddamned car. *His* goddamned car, I might add. Bought with the little money left him by his mama.

"Am I gettin down, Midge? Hell no I ain't. You can take that magic money a yours to the bank on that."

"You are a proper fool," she said, and she turned and walked off in the direction of the train.

Once she was gone, Lott climbed down from the car. He took a towel from the clothesline out front and wiped his hands and face.

"Well," he said. "She'll be back."

But after a few hours had passed and she had not come back, he decided to take a drive over to the Oquossoc station to look for her. When he got there, he parked and got out. Not seeing her on the platform or on the benches nearby, he walked over to ask if anyone had seen her board a train. He tapped a man on the shoulder and the man turned around and grinned.

"What can I do for you, friend?" he said.

He was an olive-skinned man in a three-piece suit.

"What's there some sort a convention?" Lott said.

"I'm not sure I know what you mean," the man said.

"Never mind," Lott said. "It ain't worth it."

"It is to me," the man said, and he handed Lott his card.

Lott looked at it.

Anthony Joseph Zeppa, Pinkerton Agency, Boston, MA.

"Pinkerton?" Lott said.

"That's right," the man said. "I'm looking for someone."

"You lookin for that other Pinkerton man?"

"I might be. Why don't you tell me what you know about him?"

~

Morgan burst into Barker's office.

"What do you know about the boy with the broken neck?" he said.

"Sorry, Mr. Barker," said the bartender, following in tow. "I tried to stop him—"

"Come, come," Barker said. "Sit down, Agent Morgan. Gabriel, it's quite alright."

"I'm not sitting," Morgan said, "until you tell me what the hell's going on."

Barker nodded at the bartender who took his cue and walked out.

"Will you please sit," Barker said. "Marlow here gets uppity when people make a scene."

The dog sniffed at the air.

"I just came from a scene," Morgan said. "A crime scene. And unless you tell me what's going on—*exactly* what's going on—I'll have no choice but to notify the police. I can't cover up a homicide."

"No Agent Morgan, that won't be necessary," Barker said. "You see the authorities in these parts are under-funded and understaffed. Their operating budgets are bolstered by the goodwill and generosity of local busi-nesses, the Barker being one of them. If there's a prob-lem, I have no doubt that they'll afford us the courtesy of attempting to sort it out on our own and will only interfere if things get—how to put it?—complicated."

Barker raised his hand from his lap.

He was holding the Colt revolver.

"Now," he said. "Won't you sit down?"

Morgan sat.

"Good," Barker said. "There's a good boy. Why don't you hand me that slip of paper your little friend left in your cabin? But do it slowly. I'm old and my nerves are bad. I don't respond kindly to quick movements."

Morgan took the piece of stationery from his pocket and handed it to Barker.

It was a telegraph sent from the South Rangeley sta-tion on the day of Morgan's arrival.

It read: *Imposter spotted on inbound train. Be prepared.*

"Just as I suspected," Barker said. "Rummaging through my wastepaper basket and delivering my personal correspondences to a crook."

"He was a boy," Morgan said. "He was a goddamned child."

"Oh for Christ's sake," Barker said. "Who would've thought a conman would be so sentimental? Boys are as sinful as their fathers, Mr. Morgan—if that is your name—and twice as cunning. Let yourself be blinded by the weakness of their frames and it's your weakness that'll be exposed."

Morgan did not react to this. Instead he said, "I saw your man on that train. He wasn't as discreet as he should've been. I hope he didn't cost you too much. I knew this was a trap before I even set foot in this creep joint."

Barker laughed.

"Funny, then, that you should walk right into it. No, Mr. Morgan, you won't pull one over on me. Not every rich man is a smart man. A good many are easy to swindle, and they deserve whatever comes to them—that's my rule. But Patton Barker will not be made a fool of. You believe yourself to be some sort of Americanized Arsène Lupin? You're a grifter. A petty thief. That's all."

"You think I do this for the money?" Morgan said. "You think I steal from you and men like you for profit?"

"What else?" Barker said. "Plutus is man's true God. In wealth we live and move and have our being."

"I do it because you're powerless to stop me," Morgan said. "I do it because I can."

Barker smiled.

"On my signal," he said, "a real Pinkerton agent will come through that door, one who has worked undercover for me for several years. Someone I know. Someone I trust. Someone whose identity you could never take."

"I look forward to meeting him," Morgan said.

"I wouldn't if I were you," Barker said. "This meeting will be your last."

Then he whistled.

The door creaked open and in walked the wife of Eddie Fontane, a gun in each hand.

"You see," Barker continued. "I recognized her potential years ago. She'd been orphaned and was running with a rough crowd, a group of lowlife hoodlums like you. I alone saw her talent. I saved her. I contacted one of my friends at the Pinkerton Agency and he was good enough to take her in. He cared for her. He trained her. He put her to work. And when it became clear that Eddie Fontane saw himself as my rival, I called in a favor and had her assigned to the case. She convinced him that she'd marry him, but in reality, she's been working for me ever since."

Morgan smiled.

He stood and walked over to the bookcase by the hearth.

"A group of lowlife hoodlums like me?" he said.

"What do you think you're doing?" Barker said.

"I'm admiring your books."

Morgan scanned the shelves until he found what he was looking for and pulled down a slender metal box which had been wedged between the volumes of Plato. He opened it. Inside was a thin, aged pamphlet, dog-eared and brittle.

"Don't touch that," Barker said. "That book is very rare."

"I know," Morgan said. "We've been looking for it."

Barker turned to the redhead.

"Make him put it back," he said. "Then shoot him."

"Take a look, dear," Morgan said. "We found it."

He took the pamphlet from the box and carefully turned the worn pages.

"Shoot him!" Barker said.

But instead of shooting him, the girl turned the guns on Barker himself.

"What's this?" Barker said.

"Mr. Barker," Morgan said as he carefully placed the pamphlet back in the box. "We'll be taking this."

Barker looked at the girl with surprise.

"You?" he said.

She winked and gave him a devilish smile.

"I didn't know you were so fond of my childhood sweetheart," Morgan said. "As it turns out, I'm still taken by her myself."

~

As the livery car made its way through the woods down the dirt road to the Barker, Lott smelled the smoky smell of campfires. The sun had nearly set over the lake but the orange glow of the last rays of an August day seemed to illuminate the horizon and light the world afire with a flame unmade, a sacred light that would still be burning long after the world had burned itself out.

"What in the hell?" said the Pinkerton agent sitting in the passenger seat of Lott's car.

"I'll be goddamned," Lott said as the car pulled around a corner and began rolling down the gentle slope that led to the Barker.

In front of them, the main building of the resort was engulfed in flames, fire like the salivating tongues of so many devils licking the corners, the rooftop, the windows, leaping out of doors. The livery car rolled to a stop and Lott and the man calling himself Agent Anthony Joseph Zeppa got out and joined a crowd of people on the lawn in front of the burning building.

"What happened here?" the Pinkerton man said.

But no one answered, so fixed were they on the flames.

"What happened?" he said.

Then Eddie Fontane spoke. "I take it someone finally outwitted old man Barker, though it couldn't have been easy. He's as cunning as the serpent and twice as slick. Someone patient, willing to wait for things to come rather than trying to seize them all at once. I don't suppose anyone could've done it alone. He probably needed the help of his friends, a whole chorus of friends, a sacred brotherhood rallying together in service of their cause. Those friends must've despised the old miser too and everything he stood for and the whole world he'd built. Who that gang of outlaws might be, I can't say. But it's good to see the geezer knocked down off his horse. It's been a long time coming. And I'm sure that whoever did it is having a good laugh at this misadventure and all the destruction it's brung with it."

With that, Fontane walked off into the darkness whistling a jaunty tune.

Suddenly, the onlookers became aware of the sound of footsteps approaching from out back, the crunching of leaves under leaden feet. Old man Barker emerged from somewhere behind the blaze, as pale and as lifeless as a corpse. He was stunned and babbling and he fell on his knees in front of the crowd of onlookers.

The bartender Gabriel ran to his aid.

"My dog," Barker was saying. "My dog. My dog."

"What is it, sir?" the bartender said.

"My dog," Barker said. "That black bastard made off with my dog."

~

There was no one on the 9 o'clock train departing from the Oquossoc station. No one but them.

The train started up and rolled down the tracks.

Morgan looked out the window at the sprawling blueberry fields, the white moon transfiguring everything with light.

He turned and looked at her, stroked her soft, auburn hair, touched his hand to her porcelain cheek.

She nestled her head into his shoulder.

"Next stop, South Rangeley Station," the conductor called.

Morgan looked back out the window.

"There it is," he said.

"Where?" she said.

"That tree right there," he said. "And the house was right over here by the tracks."

She closed her eyes and hugged him tight, his body too big to hold.

He took the Colt revolver from his jacket pocket and placed it under his waistband. Then he pulled a box of matches from his coat and lit the cigar he had commandeered from old man Barker's private humidor. He blew a plume of white smoke into the air and tapped the ash onto the floor.

Some of the soot landed on the dog at his side and the animal began to growl.

Morgan whacked it with the back of his massive hand.

The dog whimpered and curled up next to him, pressing its face into his side.

"Good boy," Morgan said. "That's a real good boy."

He placed the cigar in a nearby ashtray, pulled a thin metal box out from under his seat, and opened it. He couldn't read a word of Greek, but he knew just what he was holding. A book that contained all the mysteries of existence. A book that could tell him who he was.

"Stes'll be happy," the girl said with a yawn.

"Yes," Morgan said. "I do believe he will."

The two of them closed their eyes. The dog lowered its head. And before long, they were all fast asleep.

Part Two

The Man Who Was Sunday

nthony Joseph Zeppa cared about his appearance. The way things look, he knew, often matters more than the way things are. As the curator of a specially-formed unit of the Pinkerton Agency—that emblem of American freedom which, by its very existence, proves that freedom is secured with deception—he was accustomed to wearing masks made of other men's faces. His job was to stoop and hide, to present himself one way and all the while be another—and, more than that, to identify and recruit those who could do the same. So, as he walked through the cobblestone streets near Cornhill on a bright June morning, tapping his cane, clicking the heels of his shoes, and whistling a jaunty little tune, he concealed himself behind the flamboyant dress of a violet three-piece suit, crisp starched shirt front, spotted floral necktie, formal black dress gloves, and costly homburg hat. And, looking thoroughly out of place, he attracted the attention—not to say, the ire—of more than one pale Massachusetts puritan who looked at the short, clean-shaven Italian with his haughty getup, thick, Roman nose, and olive complexion with the kind of disdain reserved for immigrants who are not merely immigrants but also, undoubtedly, papists.

The Sunday morning service was just letting out at King's Chapel and the faithful were flocking into the street. At first, everything seemed to be as it should, the women leading the children out front, the men waiting respectfully by the door; but a closer look suggested to Zeppa that something was amiss. There was a mur-

mur rising up among the congregants, a cacophony of hushed voices and startled expressions. One of the children was green and whining that he was ill. His mother was flushed in the face. She sat down on the curb and began to groan and mutter that she was dizzy. Another woman put her hand to her temple and collapsed back into her husband's arms. There was a boy vomiting in the doorway and people were beginning to push and shove their way out into the adjoining churchyard, coughing and heaving as they went.

Noticing this, Zeppa stopped in the shade of a nearby yew, took a cognac-dipped cigarillo from his smoke-box, lit it, blew a plume of white smoke into the air, and waited to see what would happen. He could hear a man crying in a tear-choked voice, "Poison! We've been poisoned with the elixir of the devil!" and saw the pastor come barreling out with a crazed look in his eye.

More people were vomiting now and some of the women were in hysterics.

Zeppa puffed on his cigarillo, dropped it to the ground, stepped on it, and approached.

"Good morning, Reverend," he said with an affable grin. "What seems to be the issue?"

The pastor looked up at him, bewildered.

"You are the Reverend Breen, are you not? The famous Boston teetotaler?"

The man had a frothy white foam dribbling down his chin.

Zeppa reached into the pocket of his velvet suitcoat and pulled out a silver flagon.

"There's nothing that exercises the demon like a little more," he said and offered the churchman a drink.

The pastor bent forward and began heaving.

Zeppa shrugged, lifted the flask to his lips, and ripped off a hearty swig.

There was a tug on his coat sleeve.

He turned and saw a boy standing before him.

"Wilkins," he said in a cheerful voice.

"I think it worked," Wilkins said.

Zeppa looked around at the drunk and stupefied laymen.

"Yes," he said. "I think it did."

"Well," said Wilkins. "Where's my pay?"

"Your pay?" said Zeppa. "Isn't a good laugh its own reward?"

"It can be," Wilkins said. "But I want to be paid all the same."

Zeppa sighed.

"Ok," he said. "A deal's a deal."

He took a quarter eagle from his pocket and held it out.

The boy lunged for it.

Zeppa pulled it away.

"Now just a minute," he said. "Where's the rest of that grain?"

"None left," Wilkins said. "I mixed it all into their juice."

"Wilkins," Zeppa said. "Don't lie to me."

The boy hesitated.

"Well," he said. "I might a kept a bit for myself."

"A bit?" Zeppa said.

"Just a sup," Wilkins said.

"Ok," Zeppa said. "Consider it a bonus for a job well done. Only next time, don't think you can hide it from me."

"No sir," Wilkins said. "Ain't nothin gets by you."

Zeppa smiled and rubbed the boy's hair.

"Here you go," he said and handed him the gold coin. "You've earned it."

The boy took the coin, examined it, and bit it with his teeth.

"It's real," Zeppa said. "What do you think I am?"

"I know what you are," Wilkins said. "It's why I checked."

Zeppa laughed.

"Go on," he said. "Before these proper churchmen come to their senses and realize they're the butt of your little joke."

"Now it's my joke?" Wilkins said.

"Who else's?" Zeppa said.

"You know who else's," Wilkins said. "Yours."

"Well, who performed it?"

"You're like that man at the fair," Wilkins said. "The one with the bowtie."

"Bowtie?" Zeppa said.

"Yeah," Wilkins said. "He throws his voice behind these little dummies and makes em talk."

"He's a ventriloquist," Zeppa said.

"Not him," Wilkins said. "You."

"Very well," Zeppa said. "But you're no dummy."

"No," Wilkins said. "But sometimes I play the part."

The boy examined the coin once more before putting it in his pocket.

"Hurry along," Zeppa said. "These people won't like to know that they're being laughed at."

"It'd do em some good," Wilkins said. "That's what they call humility."

"I think you're right," Zeppa said. "In fact, I know you are."

The boy turned and began to walk off toward the city center.

"Oh Wilkins," Zeppa called after him.

The boy stopped and looked back.

"You be careful with that hooch," Zeppa said. "It's strong stuff."

The boy nodded and walked off.

Zeppa turned back to the pastor who was still hunched forward expelling his insides out onto the grass at his feet.

"You hear that, Reverend?" he said. "You listen to that boy's sermon on humility? Who'd a thunk such wisdom could come from the mouth of a babe?"

When Zeppa arrived, he found the jailer sitting in chains out front and the police commissioner waiting to greet him.

"O'Meara," he said, and he tipped his hat.

"Zep."

"Your boys inside trying to piece together what happened?"

"We know what happened," the commissioner said. "We just don't know how."

"And that's why I'm here?"

"You're here because you have a knack for sorting these things out."

"I'm touched," Zeppa said. "Why don't you tell me what you know."

"Well, this drunk sonofabitch had something to do with it," the commissioner said, and he gave the jailer a kick.

"I may be a drunk," the jailer said. "But I ain't no scoundrel."

Zeppa bent down and looked the man in his sallow, sunken eyes.

"With all due respect," he said, "that's not for you to say."

"And just who in the fuck're you supposed to be?" the jailer said.

"I'm the man who gets to decide what you are," Zeppa said, and he stood back up.

"We're not sure why he did it," the commissioner said. "Or even what he did. But there's no other explanation. A man doesn't just turn into a lady over night. And certainly not such a lovely one while we're at it."

"There are other possibilities," Zeppa said.

"Such as?"

"Have you considered sorcery?"

"Be serious," the commissioner said.

"I am serious," Zeppa said. "Why not? Read a book from any century save our own and you'll see that we're the anomaly in eschewing such answers."

"Don't talk smart to me," the commissioner said. "And don't dress up your buffoonery to sound smart neither."

"I was visited by a wizard," the jailer said, and he hiccupped.

"Shut up, you," the commissioner said.

"I ain't lyin," the jailer said. "It was a wizard. Or maybe," and he hiccupped again, "a priest, which is really the same damn thing."

"I'm warning you," the commissioner said.

"Now hold on a minute, Stephen," Zeppa said. "Let's hear him out."

"He's just taking jabs because I'm Irish," the commissioner said.

"I ain't jabbin at you you mick bastard," the jailer said.

Zeppa laughed.

"It's the only one been in or out a that cell in two months," the jailer said.

"Who is?" Zeppa said.

"Who're we talkin about?" the jailer said. "That priest."

"You let a priest in?" Zeppa said.

"Yeah," the jailer said. "Friar Somethin. Can't remember his name. Came about two weeks back."

"Why'd you let him in?" the commissioner said.

"Well," the jailer said. "You said it yourself. I'm weak for drink."

Zeppa rubbed his chin. Then he looked at the commissioner.

"Ok," he said. "Take me to see her."

"What?" the commissioner said. "No more questions for the man who done it?"

"No," Zeppa said. "I already know the whole story."

~

The cell in which they had kept the Roman was small and dank, hardly big enough to fit the cot on which he'd slept. It was located at the far end of the prison, separate from the lodgings of the other inmates, and you had to pass through two locked doors to access it. It was typically reserved for the most violent of criminals, those for whom life had become nothing more than a waiting, a counting of the hours until they would be hung by their necks. In the case of the Roman, however, an exception was made. Though he had physically harmed no one, he had exercised a kind of violence against the commonwealth unmatched by any mere murderer—or so the prosecutor had argued. In making a mockery of the state, of its institutions, its customs, and its laws, he had undermined its authority, attacked its integrity, and sowed the seeds of the worst kind of anarchism—not the kind which, in its desperation, resorts to the throwing of bombs, but an anarchism of the mind, a dissatisfaction with the nature of things, a rebellion against the world itself.

"Good day, miss," Zeppa said, and he tipped his hat.

The girl standing before him in chains was no older than twenty-five, a thin, pretty girl with blue eyes and passionate red hair. She looked at him and spat on the ground at his feet.

"She's a real beaut," the commissioner said.

"Beaut yer arsehole," the girl said.

"Don't you speak to Commissioner O'Meara like that," some lackey said, and he walked toward the girl as if to intimidate her.

She lunged forward and slammed her forehead into his sternum causing him to stumble back and begin whooping and gasping for air.

"Fuck the whore who shat you out," she said.

Zeppa laughed.

"I like her," he said. "She's just my type."

"She'll be sticking around," the commissioner said. "Plenty a room for her here. But we got a figure out who she is and how she got in and how she helped the Roman escape."

"It wasn't too complicated," Zeppa said, and he smiled at the girl. "No, the question's not how, but why."

"Then you know how she did it?"

Zeppa sighed.

"Bring me the drunkard."

The lackey, who had only just caught his breath, left and returned a moment later with the jailer in tow.

"Jailer," said Zeppa. "What's your name?"

"Harris," the jailer said.

"Harris," said Zeppa. "How long was the prisoner in your care?"

"A few months," the jailer said.

"And during that few months' time, how often did you hear him speak?"

The jailer looked at him skeptically.

"I didn't help him do nothin, if that's what you're anglin for."

"Answer my question," Zeppa said. "How often did you and the inmate converse?"

"Well," said the jailer. "Not often. I'd say we didn't hardly speak at all."

"No," said Zeppa. "And when he was in this cell, what did he do?"

"What's there to do?" the jailer said. "He mostly just laid there."

"Laid here how?" Zeppa said.

"What'd you mean?" the jailer said.

"On his back? On his belly? Looking out at you through the bars?"

"No, no," the jailer said. "Facing the wall."

"Very good," Zeppa said. "And what color was his hair?"

The jailer looked at him.

"What color was his hair?"

"I can't rightly say. I think it was brown."

"Could it have been auburn?"

"It's dark in that cell," the jailer said. "You can barely see in."

"Could it have been red?"

"I'd just drop his food and walk away," the jailer said. "I didn't pay him much mind."

"Well, was it long or short? Can you tell us that much?"

"It was long. He wore it like a girl. They say that's how they do it over there, everythin all mixed up."

"So he would lay with his back to you, showing you his long hair?"

"Well, I mean ... I don't know that he was showin it."

"Oh he was showing it," Zeppa said. "I'd be willing to bet it was all you saw of him for the past few weeks."

"Maybe," the jailer said.

Zeppa walked over to the girl. He lifted a tress of her hair to his nose and smelled it.

"Delightful," he said.

She curtsied in mock appreciation.

"That'll be all," Zeppa said. "Take him out, unbind his hands, and fetch him a drink."

The lackey took the jailer by the arm, and they began walking down the corridor toward the exit.

"Oh Harris!" Zeppa called after them. "One last thing. That priest you let in here a few weeks back—did you happen to get a look at his hair?"

"Yeah," said the jailer. "Now that you mention it, I did."

"Long, auburn hair?"

"Long, auburn hair."

Zeppa turned to the commissioner.

"No," he said. "It's not so difficult to figure out how a thing happens. But why—that's the harder question."

~

Zeppa sat alone with the girl, smiling affably, not saying a word.

She was silent for a long while, and then finally spoke.

"Ya know I won't tell you where he is, don't ya?"

"I know," he said. "You wouldn't be worth much to him if you did."

"Then what're we doing?"

"What are we doing?" Zeppa said and he went on smiling.

The girl looked at him uncomfortably.

"Why don't I tell you some other things I know? I know all about your little plan and just what it took to execute it. I know you came here dressed as a friar, bribed your way in with booze, entered the Roman's cell, exchanged your garbs for his, allowed him to exit as if he were you, and remained unseen for weeks by fixing your face to that wall and letting no one see anything save the back of your head."

She shrugged.

"I know he wanted to get caught. The whole point was for him—or rather, you—to be in here while he was out there so no one would know what he was up to, the mischief he was making."

She glared at him.

"But I know what he was up to. I know the mischief he was making. And that means I don't need you to say a word."

"You don't know yer arsehole from a bunghole."

"Let's see what I know and what I don't. I know that you're not from overseas and that that accent is as fake as the beard you wore when you entered this place."

"Good," she said. "I was getting tired of using it."

"I know that you know the Roman well, that you've worked with him for years under various names and guises—though he still has a few masks of which you're unaware. I know he's won your loyalty and that you wouldn't betray him no matter how many disadvantages that loyalty brings with it."

She looked at him intently.

"I know that he's responsible for all kinds of mayhem, that he ruins reputations just for fun. I know he's brought down professors and politicians and public figures of every stripe, that he embarrasses them and exposes them for the false prophets they are. I know he's hated by those the world admires but loved by those it crushes, that he never ceases to entertain anyone who appreciates the tragedy at the heart of a good joke. I know he has no creed and no god, save some sort of farcical jester god who desires nothing more than to be amused, to laugh like a child, without provocation and without reserve. I know he has an army of scoundrels at his disposal, that you're one of those scoundrels, but he doesn't use you to enrich himself or bring himself glory; he's content to just undermine everything and mix everything up."

The girl began shaking and rocking herself back and forth.

"I know he pays you well and treats you better and that you'd follow him into the bowels of hell if he asked, and that in some ways—you already have."

"It can't be," she said.

He was still smiling that same, affable smile.

She took a deep breath in and exhaled.

"I don't suppose you'd give a girl like me a cigarette?"

"I only smoke cigarillos."

"It can't be," she said.

But as he took the smokebox from his jacket pocket and passed it across the table, she saw the signature S embossed on the front and knew that she too had been tricked and was sitting in the presence of her teacher and greatest friend.

"It can't be," she said.

And when she did, he winked.

~

"Do you know what the Greeks used to call the public executioner?" Zeppa said.

"Don't talk smart to me," the commissioner said.

"*Dā́mios*," Zeppa said. "The man of the people."

"You're trying to impress the wrong cop," the commissioner said. "I know everything you say can be found in a book."

"I don't care what anyone says about you," Zeppa said. "You've got brains."

"Sometimes it's advantageous to let people think of you one way and be another."

Zeppa laughed.

"Don't laugh," the commissioner said. "It's the truth."

"I only laugh at the truth," Zeppa said. "What could be funnier than the way things are?"

"I'll tell you what," the commissioner said. "The way things aren't. The way people expect them to be."

"Now who's been reading books?" Zeppa said. "You sound like a poet."

"No," the commissioner said. "I've just spent too much time around human beings, had to look too long into their madness."

"You know what the Greeks used to say about madness?"

"All right," the commissioner said. "Are you leaving or aren't you?"

"We're leaving," Zeppa said.

"Do you need an armed transport?"

"For her?" Zeppa said and he gave the girl a shove. "I may be a bit shorter and a bit stouter than a lanky old harp like you, but I wouldn't be much of a Pinkerton man if I could be outfoxed by so delicate a flower."

The girl put out her tongue.

The commissioner smiled.

"You olive eaters amuse me," he said. "I've never met an Italian who didn't fancy himself the next Machiavelli."

"The bookishness continues," Zeppa said. "I'll tell you something Machiavelli knew well. The best place to hide is in the words of others."

"Now that's sharp," the commissioner said. "Machiavelli said that?"

"Well, maybe he quoted it."

"From where?"

"I'm not sure," Zeppa said. "It must've been written by some wiseman. Perhaps someone from antiquity."

"Socrates?" the commissioner said.

"Stesichorus," the girl said.

"Stesi-what?" Zeppa said.

"Stesichorus," the girl said. "The comic poet."

The commissioner rubbed his chin.

"That doesn't sound right," he said. "I don't believe it."

"Believe what you want a believe ya prick lickin basterd."

The commissioner cocked his arm as if he were about to hit her.

The girl raised her cuffed hands to shield her face.

Zeppa shook his head.

"It's not worth it, O'Meara. She's not worth it."

The commissioner lowered his arm and spat.

"No," he said. "I don't suppose she is."

"Well," Zeppa said. "If there's nothing else, we'll be on our way."

"You really think you can get her to talk?" the commissioner said. "You think she'll tell you where he is?"

"No," Zeppa said. "But I don't need her to."

"Then why are you taking her?"

"I'm going to use her," Zeppa said. "To set a trap."

The commissioner smiled.

"Do me a favor," he said.

Zeppa nodded.

"Bring him to me first—when you catch our white whale."

"I will," Zeppa said. "Before this story's done, I'll walk that Roman bastard right into your office. You have my word on that."

"Unbar the door!" the commissioner called and at the far end of the hall, the lackey unlatched and opened the front door.

"Follow me, dear," Zeppa said to the girl. "And watch your step."

As they walked out into the daylight, both he and she had to raise their hands to shield their faces. Outside, birds were chirping and hopping in the trees, the sky was as clear and as blue as water, and the sun shone so bright that the green of the day was almost white, transfigured by a light both beyond this world and radiating out from it.

When he was sure they were out of earshot, Zeppa leaned in and said, "Stesichorus?"

The girl smiled.

"Why not?"

Zeppa laughed.

"Sometimes," he said, "I worry I give you too much rope. A keener ear would pick up on those things."

"Keener ears aren't so common."

"No," Zeppa said. "The ear must be trained. But so too must the mouth."

"Then train it," she said and she leaned forward and pressed her lips to his.

He pulled back and slapped her face.

"You're flirting with disaster," he said.

She rubbed her chin.

"I know just what I'm flirting with," she said. "Now get these chains off me."

"These chains are the only reason you're free," he said. "I let you out too soon and they'll throw you right back in that cell."

"No," she said. "You wouldn't let them do that."

"No," he said. "I wouldn't."

"What's next?" she said.

"We meet the others," he said. "Regroup and push on with the plan. Things are only just coming together."

"Ok," she said.

They walked a ways down the road and she said, "Hey, Stes."

"Yeah?" he said.

"I didn't like that you hit me."

"No," he said. "I didn't like it either."

The gang was known by many names, but they called themselves the King's Chorus. They were a band of misfits, lawless young scoundrels who took nothing seriously, not even their lives. Most men can be bought. Others fear condemnation. But those who laugh at the riches of the world and laugh louder at its threats are a dangerous brood. They're dangerous not so much to one another nor even to themselves—what, after all, can be taken from those who give everything away?—but to the order of things, the stability of human affairs, the structure of daily life. They're a scourge upon society, a blasphemy against its rights, an insult to its privileges. Sitting in judgment of its judgments, defying its demands, they stand as a perpetual finger in the eye of the city of man and by their insolence, reveal its true nature. They say, *I will not take you seriously, no matter how seriously you take yourself.* They say, *Isn't all this seriousness just a game? A pretense, a farce, a play put on for others?* They say, *I may be a fool, but my folly is wiser than your wisdom and your wisdom is your folly, no more than a chasing of the wind.* They say, *How ridiculous you are, and how cowardly, and how weak—is that why you insist upon reverence?* They say, *Live like me, find freedom in frivolity, and be done with all the rest; your suffering will increase, but so too will you learn to laugh—man's greatest triumph.* Looking the powers of the world in the eye, they neither cower nor bow. They smile—and are condemned for it. What greater sin can there be than to bless where other men curse?

How the King's Chorus came to be and why is still a mystery. There are legends told about its founding and much has been written about what it set out to do. There are those who condemn its buffoonery and those who would canonize its members, those who advocate for the suppression of this story and those who emulate the mischief-makers depicted therein. I won't recount any of that here; nor will I indulge the curiosity of the reader who wishes to peer down into mysteries from a distance without purifying himself by dirtying his hands. All I will say about the Chorus—or the Lords and Ladies of Misrule, or the Children of Momus, or Aesop's Asses, or the Clouds, or the Philosopher Queens, or Cordelia & Company, or the Fire Blight Society, or Trimalchio's Minions, or the Squires of Faith, or Memnon's Marauders, or whatever else men have called them—I will say because it directly pertains to the matters at hand. But should the reader, inspired by that most lamentable of concupiscences—the curiosity of the eyes, the desire to see that which ought not to be seen and know that which cannot be known—should the reader wish to hear more about this mirthful band of merrymakers and sots, well he'll have to sate his desire elsewhere. I will not pull back the curtain, no matter how much he begs.

The Chorus was waiting for Zeppa and the girl—whose name, by the way, was Persephone Finn, granddaughter of the Irish playwright Rory Finn, who was shot through the head by a representative of the Crown for being drunk and unruly back in the old country one St. Cecilia's Day 1878—in a grimy tavern on a stonelaid road by the harbor. These were the early days, though not so early, since Zeppa had been employed by the Pinkertons for some time and had, relying upon the air of legitimacy such organizations bestow, already assembled quite the chorus. The group was smaller then, less accomplished and less well known. I can't say how many members were at the Masked Reveler's Tavern that afternoon, but I know Lionel Oats was there, who would, years later, die in a gunfight outside of Kansas City, and so was Tomas Zurita, who became famous for kidnapping and then impersonating a state senator in order to push a number of significant bills through the Rhode Island legislature. Jasmin Janson may have been there, who transformed the field of Christology when, dressed as a man, she gave a series of important lectures on Luke 24 at the Andover Theological Seminary. Herman Harmon must have been there. Let's assume he was. And so too must Nicholas Hornsby and Natasha Limon have been in attendance.

Now, after reading the conversation that follows, you may end up wondering how much of what is written is true and to what extent you can rely upon my representation of the dialogue that took place at the tavern that afternoon. In defense of the exactitude of my retelling, I bring forth none other than Zeppa himself, who, as you shall see, will soon insist that "nothing is true except what is written." The clever reader will perhaps take issue with this and argue that Zeppa could not have meant what he said since he never wrote a word and went to extraordinary lengths to make sure that his deeds were neither discovered nor recorded. Well, clever reader be damned. What good is a clever reader when he lacks the requisite faith to appreciate a simple story told in earnest by the man who lived it? No, I beseech you—be not clever but good, be virtuous, be just, be the kind of reader who is quick to find the best in every work and magnanimous enough to overlook even the most obvious of failings. Be worthy, that is, of the story to come.

~

Zeppa balled his fist three times against the tavern's outer door.

"Who is it?" came a voice from within.

"Mrs. Grundy," said Zeppa with a wry smile hanging from his face.

The door swung open before him and in he walked followed by the girl in chains.

"Get me the bolt croppers," she said as she stepped into the light of the bar.

"Now, dearie," said one member of the Chorus. "What fun would that be for all of us? Maybe we'll keep you in them cuffs for a while. I know some good party games we could play."

"That'd be nice," she said. "And when the party's over, I'll have some fun myself. I'll split you boys from toe to tip."

"What tip we talkin about, darling?"

She gave him a straight look.

"Right," he said. "I'll get the cutters."

Off he went and Zeppa walked over to the bar.

"Stes," said the man standing behind it.

"Lionel."

The man nodded at the girl.

"She's worth her weight in gold."

"More," Zeppa said. "I hope we'll be saying the same thing about our new recruit after tonight."

"We'll see where we stand in a couple hours," the man said.

"You didn't rough him up too bad, did you?"

"Not too bad," the man said. "No worse than I was roughed up on the night you asked me to join."

"Lionel," Zeppa said. "Didn't they break one of your arms?"

"Knocked my tooth out too."

He smiled and a golden canine glittered in the barlight.

"Well," Zeppa said. "There's no avoiding pain in this life."

"No," Lionel said. "But it takes a true alchemist to turn pain into treasure."

He rubbed the tooth with his tongue and winked.

Zeppa laughed.

"Pour me two fingers," he said.

The man screwed the cap off a bottle of brown liquor and lined up a pair of glasses. He filled them, slid one to Zeppa, and raised the other in the air.

"To our new recruit."

"To our new recruit," Zeppa said. "May he live long and die laughing."

They downed their drinks.

"What do you think?" Zeppa said. "Should I keep on this ridiculous getup or show myself as I am?"

"I don't know that you know yourself as you are," the man said.

"Well," Zeppa said. "I could be the Roman."

"Why trade one getup for another?"

"Then I introduce myself as the most preposterous of Pinkertons?"

"If the dandy suit fits."

"It's not too much?" Zeppa said.

"Too much?" the man said. "What's that even mean?"

"Very well," Zeppa said. "Let's round everyone up. Tell them to meet me in the cellar in five minutes."

"I'll let them know," the man said.

"And Lionel," Zeppa said.

"Yeah, Stes?"

"Make sure you bring a couple of cases down with you. I don't want to have to keep going back and forth."

"You got it, Stes."

The man walked out from behind the bar and began telling the others.

Zeppa walked to the washroom. Inside was a pot and a basin and four blank walls. The room smelled foul with human smells, and it was very poorly lit. Zeppa walked to the wall opposite the pot and pushed on the bottom of it with his foot and it lifted up as if it had hinges that fashioned the top of it to the ceiling and behind it was a stairwell that spiraled down, down into a damp cellar deep beneath the earth. Zeppa entered the passway and the door swung shut and was a wall once more and he descended the stairs, shoes clicking on the stones at his feet, clicks echoing in the darkness. When he reached the bottom, he lit a match so he could see his way and began whistling a jaunty little tune. The tune took on a sinister air given the fact that a man was being held captive in that basement and he had been beaten and was bleeding and he feared that the approaching footsteps belonged to his executioner come to exact upon him the sentence bequeathed by those with the power to bequeath it. But when Zeppa entered the room in which the man was being held and lit a gas lamp with his match, the man saw the violet suit and spotted tie and bulbous Roman nose, and he knew not what to make of so bizarre and singular an apparition.

Zeppa smiled.

Morgan spat on the ground at his feet.

"Now," said Zeppa. "Is that any way to treat the man who would set you free?"

~

Not long after that, Lionel entered carrying three crates filled with wine and whiskey and the rest of the Chorus followed in tow.

"Cut off those ropes," Zeppa demanded. "This man is our guest."

And before Morgan knew it, he was untied and on his feet and had been fed enough whiskey to pacify a small horse. The Chorus regaled him with chants and drinking songs and one played the fiddle and another the flute and the room lit up with stories and reveries and laughter. Morgan didn't understand what was happening, but he knew he was in the company of friends, and he let himself go in a way he had not been able to since he was a boy. The whole time, Zeppa smiled at him and he felt the warmth of that smile and at one point, emboldened by the comradery and by the drink, he walked across the cellar and asked one of the members of the Chorus if he might steal a dance and she nodded and Morgan took her by the hand and asked her her name and she said Persephone and he spun her around the room with such grace and such buoyancy that they appeared to be floating rather than dancing, rising up from this underworld to a life as light as vapor and yet more sacred. He spun her around and around and her red hair glowed in the light of the lanterns and when the music stopped, he set her down and kissed her hand and retired to the corner where someone fed him another drink and he laughed and watched the others still dancing.

When everyone was drunk and in the mood for conversation, the flute playing died off and Lionel and some others pulled chairs from a closet and arranged them in a big circle, and everyone sat and began to make toasts and speeches. Much of what was said was drunken blather and there was a good deal of hiccupping, but some of the talk pertains to our story and the whole reason for introducing the Chorus and recounting this tale was to shine a new light upon our friend Morgan and upon his motives and what led him to the Barker in August 1908, so I'll focus on the parts that are significant and leave out the rest.

"Stes you are a spectacular ass!" Herman Harmon said.

"Why thank you," Zeppa said, and he leaned forward in his chair as if to bow.

"No, no, I mean it," Harmon said. "I've never met someone as brilliant and as foppish as you, and always both at the same time."

"Here, here," Zurita said, and he lifted the bottle from which he was drinking in mock toast.

Persephone raised her glass as well and soon everyone's drink was in the air, and all were cheersing and gulping.

"That's it! That's it!" Lionel said. "That's just what we need. A roast."

"A roast?" said Nicholas Hornsby.

"A roast," Lionel repeated. "And Stes will be the pig."

"Now," said Zeppa and he nodded at Morgan. "What's this got to do with our friend here? He's the guest of honor, after all."

"It's got everything to do with him," Lionel said. "Hell, he doesn't even know who you are, let alone what you want him for."

"That's true," Zeppa said.

"Well, what better way to introduce you?"

"Yes, let's roast him," Zurita said. "And I'll start."

"No, me!" said Oskar Frump.

"I want to go first," said Mona Deville.

"There's only one way to decide," Lionel said. "Our guest should choose."

"Me?" Morgan said.

"You," Lionel said. "Who here looks like a reliable chap?"

"Or dame!" Persephone added.

"Or dwarf!" shouted Richard Leech.

"Oh fuck off you Lilliputian bastard," Lionel said. "You weren't excluded for being short. You've got red blood and a pecker, don't you? You're as much of a chap as any of us."

"More of one," said Leech. "And don't you forget it."

"Well," Morgan said as he looked around the room. "I don't really know any of you. But for some reason I trust you all."

"You have to choose," Lionel said.

Morgan's eyes circled the room and finally landed on the girl with the red hair.

"Persephone," he said.

She smiled.

"I choose you."

"Well," she said. "You've chosen right. I don't think anyone here's known Stes as long as I have, and I doubt anyone knows him so good."

Zeppa nodded in agreement.

"But it's not just Stes I know. It's everyone in this room. Even you Mr. Morgan."

Morgan looked at her, perplexed.

"You see, I've worked with Stes for a very long time. Since I was a girl, really. You might even say that it was with him that my life began. Before that, I ran with a pretty rough crowd. We were a group of lowlife cons, nothing but a bunch a two-bit swindlers. We ran our grift out of south Maine. Most of us were orphans or runaways, kids who'd been knocked down by the world and were determined to knock it back again."

Morgan's eyes lit up. He looked at the girl as if seeing her for the first time.

"I remember this one little hooligan—Knuckles we called him. Wouldn't stop fightin until his hands ran with blood."

"It can't be," Morgan said.

"It is," she said. "I told you, Mr. Morgan. I know you. I've known you for a long time."

"You're—"

"One and the same," she said. "When I last saw you, you were just a boy. You didn't know how to talk to a girl, let alone dance with one. Now look at you. Big as a man and able to play the part."

"It can't be," Morgan said.

"Why don't I tell you how I got here?" she said. "How all of us got here? How you got here? And what's going to happen next."

Morgan couldn't tell if he was drunk or dreaming or some combination of the two, but he knew that whatever this was, it wasn't his life. Unlike in books, in life—things don't fit together. The fragments aren't pieces of a puzzle. They can't be properly arranged or put in their right places. Life is nothing but shards of broken glass, except there was no vase and no one knocked it on the floor.

"Stes is a monstrous ass," the girl said. "And something worse besides. He's friends with all of us. In this room you have crooks and bandits, whores and cheats and good-for-nothing scoundrels. But—and this is the God's truth if there is one—not one of us is a born criminal. No, the law made us sin. Or at least the men who made the law. The decent ones. The respectable ones. The ones who say what's right.

"Now, if this was a real roast, I suppose I'd start by laying into some of my fellow roasters. I'd make a crack about Perceval's first trip to the brothel, how his mother scolded him for bothering her at work; or I'd tell you about Violet's problem with the drink, that she can't hold her liquor . . . without having to down it; or I'd call little Richard here "Dick Leech" and then tell a truish story that made sense of the name."

"Fuck your mother!" Leech said.

"You would," Persephone said. "You necrophilic imp."

"The cheek on this one," Leech said. "She needs a good slap."

"I'll get the stepstool," Lionel said.

Leech laughed into his drink.

"But this isn't a roast," Persephone continued. "Not really. So I'll tell you the truth about Stes as best as I know how. I'll focus on what's important and leave out the rest."

(At this point, I suspect the clever reader I mentioned above will pause, pull out his trusty blue pen, underline Persephone's words, and write a note in the margin referring back to page 69 because the previous sentence seems to echo something I said only a few pages ago. Well, such a reader is, in truth, too clever for his own good. For, in believing to have found me out, he has inadvertently exposed himself. Yes, he may be clever, but he is far from careful. You see, the careful reader—the exceedingly careful reader—will have realized that although my narration precedes Persephone's in the text, hers precedes mine in the world and, in telling her story, I'm only retelling it; my words are an echo of hers.)

"When I first met Stes," the girl said, "he was as eccentric as he is now but not quite as brazen. Success has a way of emboldening you and a decade on top has made him think he's a god. Maybe he is. He's certainly closer than any man I've met. I've never seen him try his hand at anything he couldn't do and do well. He can fiddle. He can dance. He drinks all night and never gets drunk. He can ride and track and shoot. I've seen him win fistfights with boxers and barfights where he was outnumbered five to one. If he was the law, no criminal would walk free. If he was a criminal, no lawman could cage him. He can impersonate anyone and disguise himself as anything. He knows how to hide in the most obvious of places and how to appear where no one expects to see him. Just today, he revealed himself to me as a character I'd never met. Apparently, it's a mask he's worn many times without me knowing it. Agent Anthony Joseph Zeppa of the Pinkertons. Who hasn't he been?

"When he was recently arrested as the notorious conman the Roman, he prosecuted himself by playing the part of district attorney and then sentenced himself as Judge Wilhelm. He entered prison in the clothes of a convict and walked out the front door wearing the garbs of a humble priest. Then he came back not two weeks later dressed as this gaudy shamus you see before you only to walk out again with me at his side. Men with a third of his talent and none of his wit spend their whole lives trying to get noticed. He's content not to let anyone know his name. His greatest deeds are done in silence, inside jokes for him and friends. Yet he keeps some even from his friends and we only find out what he's been up to years later, like he's been laughing without us the whole time.

"None of this is meant as a compliment. All of it is true. And I'm telling you because I want you to understand just how strange, just how startling, just how marvelous the man who brought you here really is. Stes is the most singular, the most surprising, the most unnatural man who's ever lived. There's something inhuman about him. Something unreal. As if he's not from this world. As if he's come from beyond it just to disrupt it and mix everything up. He doesn't care about money. I've seen him leave a chest full of banknotes untouched even though we were alone, and its owner was dead, and nobody knew it existed and nobody would've known if we took it. He's not concerned with comfort and even invites pain if it means getting what he wants. He's never bored. He's never anxious. He rarely loses his temper. He's not bothered when things go wrong. He plans for them to. He accepts things as they come and acts surprised and delighted when they go right.

"He's hand-selected each of us, called us all by name. And now he wants you to join his chorus. None of us knows why. But we all know that if you do, you'll be in for a hell of a good time. Your life will become harder and more agonizing and more preposterous and more hilarious than you ever thought possible. But you'll never want it to be any other way again. So the question, Knuckles, is: Will you join us?"

Before Morgan could speak, Zeppa turned to him and said, "Don't believe anything Persephone told you. Remember, this is a roast. The point is to make me look like a fool. I think we can all agree that our redhaired friend has done a fine job of that, though she's made herself sound a bit mad in the process. In truth, however, I'm no great man. If I was, wouldn't you have heard my name somewhere before? No, I think of myself as something of a cheery minor poet, a man who likes to have a bit of fun and enjoys a good laugh when in the company of friends and compatriots. Of course, I've never written anything and none of my poetry appears in print. That's because the truest verse is not written but lived. And the true poet is at one with his art.

"You, Mr. Morgan, are a man who's written himself into existence. I've followed your exploits, though you've tried to keep them hidden, and I admire the feats you've pulled off. It takes bravado to impersonate a Pinkerton man. And stealing from the men you've stolen from takes something more than that. The problem is, you think yourself clever. You're proud of what you've done. It's a mistake. The bigger you are, the smaller your work. If you want to keep robbing trains, taking a bit here and a bit there—go ahead. That'll be a life for you. But I have it on good authority that you want something more. I know what Patton Barker and his associates stole from you all those years ago and I suspect that somewhere in the secret recesses of your heart, you've prepared a finer work just for him. Hell, that rich bastard has just about commissioned it.

"Well, if you want to learn how to make real music, if you want to write immortal poems, write them with your life. It's time to let go of yourself for the sake of your art. Join our humble chorus. It's true, you'll have to give up a bit of your originality. Instead of being the singular character you are you'll have to become just one among many. But so too will you find friends with whom you can share your work, friends who understand the joke. And that's worth more than you know. Because it's hard not to sneer when laughing alone; but with friends, even scorn turns to laughter."

"What is it you want me to do?" Morgan said.

"When was the last time you were back home in Rangeley?"

"I haven't been back," Morgan said. "Not since I was a boy. Not since the night my boyhood was taken from me."

"Well, as it turns out," Zeppa said, "I have some friends in that area. Some people who also think it's time for Patton Barker to get his comeuppance."

Morgan looked at him with surprise.

"I'm one of them," Persephone said. "And you'll recognize the name of another. Eddie Fontane."

"You work with Eddie Fontane?" Morgan said.

"To be honest," Zeppa said. "Barker is small potatoes to me. But he's important to you. And he's important to Persephone. And Eddie has his reasons for hating him. And I—well, I happen to know he's in possession of something that matters a good deal to me and that he intends to sell it to a man who matters to me even more. And that's something I simply cannot abide."

"Mr. Morgan," Persephone said. "How would you like to be in on an inside joke?"

Part Three

An Ending . . . of Sorts

"Whoever done that to Mr. Barker," the livery-man said, "he sure is goin to get it."

Zeppa looked out the window of the car as it rattled down the dirt path and did not say a word.

"Because let me tell you, Agent Zebra, that Patton Barker is not a man to be messin with. He runs these parts. Runs more than that far as I'm concerned. He's got money is what I'm sayin. And in this world, money means power. It means a lot a things besides. Means tellin a man like me 'do this' and you damn well better believe I'm goin to do it. How else is a liveryman supposed to make his livin? That's all I aim to do. Live. Got the word right there in the title. Well, what's it mean? Far as I can tell, it means scrappin just to survive. It means takin what's bein offered and bein grateful to have it. That's what those halfwit churchy types don't understand. They think it don't cost you nothin to be good. 'My yoke is easy' and all that hogwash. Well, I never known a yoke to be easy. Except the over easy kind. That's the Mrs.'s specialty right there. Eggs over easy and a buttermilk biscuit. At least it used to be—that is until this mornin. I have no clue where that woman run off to. And to be honest, I'm not so sure I care. Except I do worry. That's what it is to take a vow. It's what you sign up for, I suppose. A lifetime a worry. What do you do with that? I'll tell you what you do. You find yourself a bottle or you find yourself a gun. I've tended to opt for the former. But these days I've been thinkin, maybe it's time for another way. Better well-hanged than ill-wed. That's what mama always used to say."

Zeppa laughed.

"You like that one?"

The man smiled a big, toothy smile.

"Yeah I got a whole bunch. That's what you do with phrases. Collect em. Then you put em out there and let people enjoy what they hear or miss it altogether. Either way, it don't matter much. Just need to know how to pay attention is all. How to stay alert, that is. Which ain't always an easy thing to do. So many things get in the way. A lot a noise in this life, that's what pa used to say. A lot a nonsense is what it is. Keep you from seein what's right in front a you. Take old man Barker, for instance. How'd someone pull the wool over his eyes? That man sleeps standin up from what I hear. Plus he got the devil on his side. And the devil don't sleep a wink. The book calls him the prince a this world, but I tend to think he's the author. A second-rate author at that. And a fourth-rate thinker besides. But still, he's got his points. Knows how to spin a yarn is what I'm sayin. Always mixin things up and makin em run about in funny designs. Which is what it takes to make a world like this, I suppose. Takes a touch a madness too. A sick brain and a sicker heart.

"But who's in charge, Agent Zebra? That's the question I don't have an answer to. Maybe it's God. Maybe it's the devil. Maybe nothin but time, chance, and dumb luck. Now that's a team a purblind doomsters if ever there was one. And if you can't know, how can you decide? Make choices, that is—I ask you that. You want to be on the right side a things, there's the rub. You want to do what's good and that means sidin with whoever's goin to win in the end. Well, I never been one to pick a horse. Made a lot of mistakes, is what I'm sayin. Some my fault—I'll grant you that—but a lot caused by not knowin the future. How's a man supposed to be responsible when he can't say how things'll shake out? Hell, just look at my marriage. You think I don't regret it? Don't think I don't regret it. Course there's more to it than that. Cause a all the things I regret, it's the very best one. Which doesn't sound like a compliment but I assure you—it is. Funny how a thing can sound bad when really it's good. Same happens in reverse, I suppose. Why do you think that is? Whoever made up words sure made em tricky. Like he always wanted to say two things at once. Like he wanted to say one thing but ended up sayin the opposite right along with it. What's that about? I can't rightly say. You think he just couldn't make up his mind or you think there's somethin more sinister afoot? Well, what's sinister mean? I'll tell you what it means: Just about everythin I already said. It means the devil's in charge and he knows how to get what he wants and if you ain't careful, he'll get it from you. Better to give him a little somethin to keep him off your back, that's what I say. Course once he's perched up on there, there ain't no pryin him off, no matter how much you scritch, no matter how much you beg. But why am I sayin all this? I ain't tellin you nothin you don't already know. You is a Christian man, ain't you Mr. Zebra?"

"How long is it to South Rangeley Station?" Zeppa asked.

"We ain't goin to South Rangeley Station," the man said.

Zeppa gave him a questioning look.

"If you're wantin to head off that train, best bet is to try the holdover between Bemis and Houghton. There's a little clearin in the woods where it idles for about ten minutes while the conductor gets himself some supplies."

"You know a lot about the trains."

"I better," the man said. "It's my livelihood." He laughed. "There's that word again."

"What are we going to do if we miss it?"

"It'll be there," the man said. "And Midge'll be on it. God in heaven the things that woman puts me through."

They road on in silence for another half mile before the liveryman started up again.

"You want to know one thing more about old man Barker," he said, "while we're on the subject?"

"Sure," Zeppa said.

"He's ruthless," the man said. "Ain't no man can cross him and live to tell the tale."

~

A few miles away, at a clearing in the woods, the train was stopped and idling. It was quiet outside, quiet with the unreal silence that only a fictional landscape can provide. There were no crickets chirping in the brush, no owls in the treetops above. A loon could be heard somewhere out on a lake and the train hissed and let off steam. To one standing in the woods, some lone observer with eyes to see, there was something sur-real about this vision: A metal horse made of fire and iron that snorted sparks and black smoke and charged through the country or halted on a dime, heaving in the moonlight, sighing its mechanical sighs and wait-ing stupidly for its rider to kick his spurs and thrust it onward, on into the darkness, charging at a gal-lop through meadows and farmlands, sleepy hillside towns, little villages, whole cities whose populations knew it not, saw not the harbinger of destruction, their destruction, carrying with it the disease that spread like all human things to every corner, every recess of existence, everywhere that man has set his foot or rode his horse or urged on his contraptions.

It sat there in that silence as if waiting to be seen. And there was one to see it. He approached through the bush. He ascended the stairs. He slid open the door and stepped inside.

"I," he said, "am an unexpected guest."

And he grinned at those he greeted.

~

"It's the thing about life up here," the liveryman said. "Ain't no one to help you when you need it. Got to learn how to do everythin for yourself."

"How far are we from that clearing?" Zeppa said.

"Not more than a quarter mile."

"Would it be faster if I went the rest of the way on foot?"

"Nah, it'll only take a minute. I got good at changin em."

"What did you hit?" Zeppa said.

"Hard to say," the man said. "There's rocks and ditches all over the road."

"Do you need a hand?"

"Well," the man said. "Maybe you could just come over here and hold this light."

Zeppa got down out of the car and walked back toward the rear tires. When he did, the liveryman rose to his feet. He had a shotgun in his hands. He was aiming it at Zeppa's chest.

"Bet you didn't see this one comin," he said.

"Come on, Loamma," Zeppa said. "Of course I did."

"How'd you know my name?" Lott said.

"Who do you think you're talking to?" Zeppa said. "You think I'd take a ride with a drunk bumpkin like you without knowing who you are?"

"All right," Lott said. "So you know a thing or two. But you don't know what I'm after."

"Sure I do," Zeppa said. "You've been telegraphing it this whole ride."

"Shut up," Lott said. "Let's get walkin."

"I'm afraid I don't know the way, friend."

"You walk and I'll push," Lott said, and he thrust the barrel of the gun into Zeppa's chest.

"That way?" Zeppa said.

"That's the way," Lott said.

As they walked through the woods in the dark, Zeppa thought of how much easier life would be if the world wasn't made for fools like Loamma Lott.

"You're being awful quiet back there," he said.

"Shut up," Lott said. "I'm thinkin."

"I'm thinking that whatever old man Barker is paying you, I have access to at least double. Why don't you lower that gun and let me make you richer than you dare to dream?"

"Shut up," Lott said. "The train ain't far from here."

"Mr. Barker meeting us there?"

"Oh, we're goin to have a right old party when we get there."

"Yeah? Who else is coming?"

"I thought you knew all about it."

"Well, I wouldn't say I know, but I have my guesses."

"Even you couldn't guess this."

"No?" Zeppa said. "Must be some surprise."

"Laugh all you want, court jester. But when you see who's waitin for us, you'll see why this was the only choice to make. You'll know that I'm only doin what I have to do to survive on this god-cursed boulder under the stars."

They could hear the train before they saw it, a low, dull hum that drowned out the sounds of the wilderness around them. Then they entered the clearing and saw the metal beast resting there, purring in the dark.

"Well," Zeppa said. "What would you have me do?"

"Up the stairs," Lott said. "He's waitin."

"Barker?" Zeppa said.

"Up the stairs," Lott said.

Zeppa ascended the stairs and opened the door to the first car.

Lott pushed the gun into his back forcing him inside.

The light hurt Zeppa's eyes as he entered and what he saw hurt his heart. Barker's dog lay motionless on the floor. It had been shot clear through the skull. Barker too had bled out in a horrible fashion. The dog had evidently turned on its former master and torn out the old man's throat with its jaws. Persephone had two bullet holes in her gut. She was alive, though not very. She sat blinking, propped up against the wall. Morgan was on his knees next to her, gently rubbing her brow. He had blood pouring from his shoulder and from his side, but he seemed not to notice. Lott's wife lay face down in a crimson pool and she was not moving. She had a pistol clenched tight in one hand and had been shot several times in the torso and in the head. There was a man standing at the back of the car. Thin, hairy, donning a bushy black beard and gray bowler cap, he looked at Zeppa through his round rimmed spectacles. Zeppa looked back. The man smiled and exited the car and Zeppa saw him enter the next one behind it.

"Midge!" Lott screamed.

He dropped his gun to the floor with a clank and ran to the corpse that had been his wife. He fell on his knees beside her, lifted her dead hand to his face, and began screaming. It was a shrill, piercing scream. The kind that can't be controlled. The kind that rises up out of the depths of one's being. The scream of a man brought to such a pitch of agony that he may well go insane and probably already had.

Zeppa ran to Persephone. He bent down next to her. Morgan looked at him.

"What happened?" Zeppa said.

"It was just as you said," Morgan said. "It was a setup, just like we planned. Except the dog. I couldn't control the dog. He heard Barker speak and he lost it. And once he started—everything turned to chaos from there."

"Who shot first?"

"It was that dumb bitch with the gun," Morgan said. "She didn't know how to use it."

"She came in after Barker?"

"She was the first to enter. Then Barker."

"And then what?" Zeppa said.

"Then Madrox walked in with a smile. He was smiling, the bastard. Just like you said he would be."

"Did he say anything?"

"No," Morgan said. "Not much. I pointed my gun at him and told him I ought to end him for breaking Wilkins' neck. I said we've all agreed to this life we live. We know the risk inherent in the game. But Wilkins—he was a kid. And Madrox just threw him away."

Morgan winced in pain.

"Then what happened?"

"After that, Barker started to say something, and the dog leapt at his throat. Then the cunt started shooting. She was a horrible shot. I aimed at Madrox, and he pulled out a gun and opened fire and he did not miss."

Persephone laid back and closed her eyes. She began taking short, shallow breaths and there was a gargling in her chest.

"I'll get help," Zeppa said. "You stay with her."

"No," Morgan said. "She's dying. I may be too. Forget about us."

"I'll get help," Zeppa said.

"No," Morgan said. "Get Madrox. Don't let him escape. He did this. You bring that sonofabitch down."

He took the Colt revolver from the ground at his side, put it in Zeppa's hand, and wrapped Zeppa's fingers around it.

"He did this," Morgan said. "Don't you let him get away."

Zeppa rose to his feet.

"Stes," Morgan said.

Zeppa looked down at him.

"Take this too."

He handed him the thin metal box.

Zeppa looked at it.

"It's in there," Morgan said. "We found it. Now, don't let that monster get away."

~

The gun was big in Zeppa's hand, but his hand was bigger. He held it out in front of him as he made his way from one car to the next. There were no other passengers on the train and the majority of the cars were unlit. Zeppa moved deftly through the dark. This was not the first time he had pursued an assailant on a train. The most recent adventure had ended with a hackneyed struggle to the death on the roof of one of the boxcars,

Zeppa's arms flailing wildly as his adversary choked the life out of him, saved at the last possible moment by the limb of a low hanging tree which knocked his wouldbe killer off into the mouth of a jagged ravine. It was like something out of a sixpenny novel, except it happened in the world and would never appear in print.

The train lurched forward with a jolt and Zeppa stumbled, nearly falling to the ground. The conductor had evidently returned from his nightly errands and the locomotive was once again rattling down the secluded tracks. This pursuit of Zeppa by Madrox—for surely it was Madrox who pursued, in spite of the fact that Zeppa was chasing him—this game of cat and mouse and dog and cat and man and dog and god and man, this farcical dance of wills and wits that had gone on for too long and would go on longer still, this savage rivalry and one-upmanship, this duel between unequals who could not say which was the superior and which the inferior, this play, this nonsense, this drama, this spectacle reserved only for the eyes of those who performed it, those who lived it, this challenge of all challenges, this joyful, miserable struggle, this harrowing, unending defeat, this victory of folly and absurdity, this triumph of untruth—this was all there was. Zeppa knew not when it began nor why. He had no recollection of his first encounter with Madrox. He had only ever known him as an enemy, the most bitter of foes. Sometimes he despaired of ever besting the devil. Sometimes he thought it not possible to rid the world of so charming a snake. But he had set himself this task, had chosen for himself this fate. For as long as he could remember, he had been in competition with his maker, had tried to equal him, to ensnare him and outdo him at every turn. And as he made his way through the bowels of that metal serpent coiling itself around the neck of the world, he felt surer than ever that all life could be summed up in this wicked game, all existence gleaned through the trial he now faced.

The train entered a tunnel and everything went black. Zeppa could not see the gun he held out before him, nor could he see the one pointed at his heart. Bang! Fire as red as hell and hotter hissed from the mouth of Madrox's pistol like the tongue of a salivating demon and a fist of iron punched Zeppa square in the chest. He was knocked from his feet to the floor and lay there groaning. There was no other sound. Nobody moved. The train simply rattled on and kept rolling through the wooded mountains until it reached Rumford and when it did, the body of Persephone was recovered along with those of Patton Barker and his dead dog Marlow and Loamma Lott, who had shot himself and laid sprawled out next to the bullet ridden corpse of his wife Margaret. But Anthony Joseph Zeppa was nowhere to be found, and neither was James P. Madrox. And Morgan had disappeared too, vanished as if he had never existed at all. And as far as investigators were concerned, none of them had been on the train that night and none was considered a person of interest in the investigation of the bloody ruin discovered therein. Instead, the case was filed as a mystery unsolved. And it remains that way still, awaiting the day when a worthy detective will come along and unriddle it—

Epilogue

Letter from a Boston Jailhouse

Dear Reader,

You may take it as a sign of insecurity that I feel compelled to write you in defense of the book you just read, but I assure that this brief appendage is meant neither to sway your opinion of the admittedly farcical tale you've endured nor to explain it. It has been just over six months since Zeppa and Morgan, that nefarious duo, marched me through the woods at gunpoint, made me climb into a dead man's livery car, and drove me down to Boston in chains where they turned me in to the law under the risible pretense that I was the notorious Roman of whom you have already heard. Why have I allowed myself to remain incarcerated while those scoundrels fly hither and thither like clouds on the wind? Well, as you have likely guessed, I am no fan of the *deus ex machina* and am hesitant to employ such cheap tricks, even in the service of my own freedom. Yet if you thought that the end of this story was the end of the story, I am writing to tell you it isn't. Not by a long shot. The villains may have gotten the upper hand but, as the good book says, the time is coming when there will be no more mourning or wailing or pain. Yes, I'm going to see to that—at least for myself. I'm afraid others will not be so lucky.

You see, in this tiny prison cell—four walls and a straw-filled cot—I still have my pen. I have plenty of paper too. And the pen in the hand of the author is the wand in the hand of the wizard. And the blank page is the formless void out of which God creates the heavens and the earth. With such tools, I can do more than magic. I can make finer things than the world itself.

Don't believe me? Wait and see. I promise, you have not heard the last from the man named Madrox.

Yours,
JPM
February 24, 1909, Ash Wednesday